IMAGINE

Alison Lester

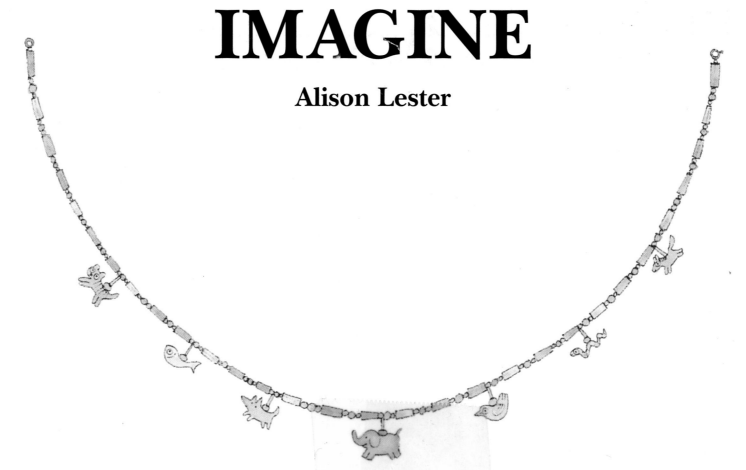

For Rich and Bee

HARCOURT BRACE & COMPANY
Orlando Atlanta Austin Boston San Francisco Chicago Dallas New York
Toronto London

Imagine
if we were
deep in the jungle
where butterflies drift
and jaguars prowl
where parakeets squawk
and wild monkeys howl . . .

■

anaconda • tree frog • paca • hummingbird • toucan • three-toed sloth • butterfly • macaw • jaguar •

scarlet ibis • butterfly

giant armadillo • peccary • cayman • spider monkey

• twist-necked turtle • water cavy • piranha • boa constrictor • howler monkey • spider monkey • cayman •

Imagine
if we were
like fish in the ocean
where anemones wave
and hammerheads glide
where seahorses rock
and hermit crabs hide . . .

■

scorpion-fish • coral • snapper • sea-cucumber • sea-urchin • cowrie • parrotfish • nudibranch • spe

nautilus • lamprey • cowrie • jellyfish • seahorse • octopus • lobster • coral

• white pointer shark • dolphin • turtle • sea-dragon • puffer fish • crab • squid • scallop • wrasse • mu

ale • hermit crab • sawfish • butterfly fish • giant clam • angelfish • angler fish • sea-snake • sponge

tusk fish • hammerhead shark • prawn • starfish • moray eel • stingray

lying fish • trumpet-fish • swordfish • flounder • moorish idol • limpet • clownfish • anemone • oyster •

Imagine
if we were
crossing the icecap
where penguins toboggan
and arctic hares dash
where caribou snort
and killer whales crash . . .

■

husky • arctic wolf • musk ox • arctic tern • snow goose • albatross • caribou • adelie penguin • sno

artic hare • adelie penguin • artic dolphin • narwhal • humpback whale

• puffin • elephant seal • emperor penguin • loon • lemming • sea lion • harp seal • guillemot • kittiwa

owl • arctic squirrel • walrus • harp seal • guillemot • kittiwake • herring • polar bear • beluga whale

killer whale • humpback whale • narwhal • arctic dolphin • arctic hare

mpback whale • narwhal • arctic dolphin • husky • adelie penguin • snowy owl • arctic squirrel • loon

Imagine
if we were
out in the country
where horses gallop
and cattle graze
where turkeys gobble
and sheepdogs laze . . .

■

bull • cow • calf • cat • kitten • stockhorse • foal • pony • draughthorse • sheepdog • puppy • sheep • g

pig • foal • goat • cockatoo • swan • cat • calf • piglet • drake • sheep • turkey

cockatoo • goat • draughthorse • sheepdog • puppy • sheep • drake • duckling • rabbit • pig • rooste

Imagine
if we were
surrounded by monsters
where pteranodons swoop
and triceratops smash
where stegosaurs stomp
and tyrannosaurs gnash . . .

◼

Imagine
if we were
away on safari
where crocodiles lurk
and antelope feed
where leopards attack
and zebras stampede . . .

∎

Imagine
if we were
alone in Australia
where bandicoots nibble
and wallabies jump
where wombats dig burrows
and kangaroos thump . . .

■

mopoke • kookaburra • wallaby • dingo • emu • numbat • rabbit • echidna • kangaroo • water-

rabbit • echidna • kangaroo • water-rat • mopoke • kookaburra • dingo

pademelon • tasmanian devil • emperior gum moth • feather-tail gilder • brushtail possum • pigmy

Imagine
if we had
our own little house
with a cat on the bed
a rug on the floor
a light in the night
and a dog at the door . . .

∎

Imagine . . .
■

This edition is published by special arrangement with
Houghton Mifflin Company.

Grateful acknowledgment is made to Houghton
Mifflin Company for permission to reprint *Imagine*
by Alison Lester. Copyright © 1989 by Alison Lester.
Originally published in Australia by Allen & Unwin
Pty. Ltd., 1989.

Printed in the United States of America

ISBN 0-15-307317-9

1 2 3 4 5 6 7 8 9 10   026   99 98 97 96